for

Emil ud

Etienne

The
Adventures of
Captain Bentley

Written and illustrated by
Mary B. Truly

To
little Mary,
you did it.

Introduction

Grace, trust and chalk dust.
Two of these I like, and one I can't seem to find.
This is the story of how I learned to trust,
let go of Grace
and draw the map to finding my true family.

Hi, my name is Bentley Fair.
I know you are probably wondering
why a ten-year-old orphan is talking about
these three odd things.
Well, the chalk dust is because I love
to draw outside on the sidewalk.
And the Grace and trust,
you will just have to wait and find out.

Chapter One

Grace

Grace, well, she is my sister,
best friend, and adventure buddy.
We pretend to travel the world
in search of the perfect place
where we can do whatever we want
and don't need anyone.
But we haven't found it yet.

In the meantime,
I go from foster home to foster home.
So far none of the families that I
have lived with have worked out.
I would get in trouble,

or I wouldn't get along with the other kids that
already lived in the family. Each time I was sent away,
I lost a little more trust in others.

Grace and I would always end up back
here at Ms. Boldmore's home for children.
It was the only place that
I have ever thought of as home.

Ms. Boldmore practically raised us along with dozens of other children. Grace and I have been with Ms. Boldmore the longest. She smells like cinnamon and always knows just what to say to help me feel better.

Chapter Two

The Tall Shadow

For as long as I can remember, I have seen a tall shadow. It has followed me to every place that I have ever lived standing in the darkness watching me.

I try to ignore it or pretend that it isn't there because it isn't really. It is a ghost or a spirit. When I have tried to look straight at it, it disappears only existing in the corner of my sight. Sometimes I can sense that it wants to tell me something, but I am too afraid of what it will say. I have never told anyone about it, not Ms. Boldmore, not even Grace. I don't trust anyone to understand. They might try to make me prove it, or they might think that I am crazy.

Grace started working at Ms. Boldmore's taking care of the orphan babies. She said that she loved it, but I could tell that she didn't. Sometimes it's like I can hear her thoughts.

I started helping out with the babies so Grace wouldn't have as much work. It became one of my favorite things to do.

Ever since I was little, Grace and I have talked about finding a place of our own. "As soon as I turn 18 we will make it happen," she would say. But as that birthday got closer, it seemed like Grace forgot our plan.

She started sneaking out at night saying that she was searching for the perfect place. I didn't believe her, but I couldn't stop her either. I would lie to Ms. Boldmore so that Grace wouldn't get in trouble.

I could tell that something was different about Grace, but she wouldn't say what was wrong. On her 18th birthday, Ms. Boldmore gave her a special box. "I've been holding on to this for you, waiting until you were old enough," said Ms. Boldmore.

That night, Grace asked to talk with me in private.
We sat in the babyroom.

"What's in the box?" I asked.
Grace opened it and
took out an old looking scroll and a key.
"A treasure map?" I asked.
"And the key to the treasure chest?"

"I don't think so," said Grace.
Then she took a letter out of the box.
"This says that the key unlocks the door to a tower."

"A tower? Where?" I asked. "What else is in the box?"
I could tell that there was more.

"Here," she said pointing to the X on the map
while ignoring my other question.
"In the middle of this island."

"Who lives there now?" I asked.

"No one lives there. The island...it belonged to our mom.
The letter says that the island and the tower are
to be passed down to us. It says here
that it is rightfully ours."

"The letter is from our mom?" I asked. Grace nodded.
She put the letter back in and closed the box.

"You can read it another time."

I couldn't believe this.
I wanted to be so happy and excited.
This should have been the best news ever,
but Grace didn't seem to feel the same way.

"Bentley, you take this."
She rolled up the map and gave it to me.
"Always keep this with you
so that one day you can find your way to me."

"You're leaving without me?" I asked.

"I've got a ride coming to pick me up tonight.
That way I can get a head start
and make the tower a nice place for us to live."

"What do I tell Ms. Boldmore
when she asks where you are?" I asked.
"I don't like lying to her."

"I think that she knows I can't stay here any longer."

"What do you mean?" I asked.

"Nothing."
Grace wouldn't meet my eyes,
but she hugged me tightly.
"Now, it's getting late. Go on to bed."

I couldn't sleep. I waited up to watch her go. I had seen Grace sneak out lots of times, but tonight I knew that she wasn't coming back.

I stayed up through the night and studied the map memorizing every inch. The tall shadow was there too, but I didn't care. I imagined that Grace would be on the island by morning safe and sound high up in the tower making it a nice place for us to live.

The next morning, when Ms. Boldmore asked me
if I knew where Grace had gone, I told her.
"Here, Ms. Boldmore. She is in the middle of this island
in a tower waiting for me. I have studied the map, and
I know where to go."

"I see..." said Ms. Boldmore.
"I think Grace needs a bit more time, dear.
Besides, I have a feeling that you should wait
until after New Parents Day to decide whether or not
you want to go and live with Grace."

"New Parents Day... that's like a month away,"
I complained stomping my foot.
I felt like Grace and Ms. Boldmore were
keeping secrets from me.

"Where have your manners disappeared to today, child?
Let's try a 'what if.' "
Ms. Boldmore said that all the time.
"What ifs" were good things to imagine coming true.
I could usually think of lots, but not today.
"I am too frustrated!" I said.

"I have a good one," said Ms. Boldmore.
"What if your perfect parents are coming?"

"My perfect parents...? I like that one," I said.

"Let's try thinking that one every day. And until then,
I could use your help with the newborns.
You are their favorite after all," said Ms. Boldmore.
"Sure," I said.
"They will need me now that Grace is gone."

Chapter Three

A Zillion Times

I used to count down the days until
New Parents Day,
wishing that a nice couple would adopt me.
But the past few years
no one even tried to talk to me
or gave me a second glance.

All the new parents cared about
were the littlest kids,
especially the newborns.

But I kept thinking my "what if" thought.
"My perfect parents are coming."
That helped a little.

But hearing all those couples cooing and awing at the baby that I had just gotten to sleep was really starting to get on my nerves. I was just about to shush them when "waahhh!" With all their noise they woke her up. Now I was angry. "Don't you people know anything... NEVER wake a sleeping baby!" I said as I came out from my hiding place.

As I calmed the baby, the new parents looked at me
as if I had three heads. I could just imagine what
they were thinking. "What a bossy child.
Someone should teach him some manners."

I went off to sit by myself.
Who would ever want to adopt me
after seeing me yell like that?
But just then...

"That was pretty impressive.
There is no way I would have been able
to stand up to all those people and calm that baby,"
said a man's voice.

I looked up and saw a couple standing in front of me.
I noticed them earlier talking with Ms. Boldmore.

"My name is Will, and this is my husband, Harry,"
said the man wearing glasses.

"My name's Bentley."

"Nice to meet you, Bentley. May we sit with you?"
asked Will.

"Sure," I said apprehensively.

Will and Harry sat on either side of me
on the window seat.

I didn't understand why they were sitting with me
and not playing with the littler kids or the babies.
I studied them.
Will seemed like he was a lawyer
or something smart like that.
Harry smelled kinda like paint and wood chips.
They both seemed nervous, which made me nervous.

"So, Bentley..." said Harry rubbing the back of his neck.
"How did you learn so much about caring for others
at such a young age? What made yo-

"Why are you two talking to me?" I asked.
I knew that it wasn't polite to interrupt people,
but I couldn't take this.
"Do you guys want me to teach you how to
take care of babies or something?"

Will and Harry gave each other a nervous glance.

"We're sorry, Bentley. Harry and I are
a little excited I guess," said Will.

"Why? What do you want?" I asked.

"We want to adopt you," said Harry.

I couldn't believe this.
"What? I mean... what?"
Ms. Boldmore would not have appreciated my
manners just then, but I didn't care.

"If you want to, we would love for you to become a
part of our family," said Will.

"Your family...?"
I dreamed about this moment a million, no
a zillion times.
Now that it was here I couldn't speak.
All I could do was smile.
I couldn't get the smile off my face.

"Is that a yes?" asked Will.

"A zillion times yes," I said.

"A zillion?" asked Harry.

"That's how many times
I have wanted this moment to come true."

Chapter Four

Trust

At the end of the day, sitting and eating the leftover cookies with Ms. Boldmore, I told her about Will and Harry and how they wanted to adopt me.

"Can you believe it, Ms. Boldmore? They aren't exactly what I expected, but they *are* my perfect parents. The thought worked!" I said.

"Yes, I can believe it," she said with a smile.

"Well I can't," I said. "I mean, I can...but what about Grace? Just when she leaves, I get adopted. Am I making the right choice? What do I do?"

"Trust that this is meant to be, my dear. Will and Harry are good people. You have been waiting for the right family for so long. You deserve to be happy."

I let out a deep breath. Ms. Boldmore always knew how to help me.

"What are they like, Will and Harry? Can you tell me about them?" I asked taking a bite of my cookie.

"Will is a history professor."

"Harry is a carpenter and an artist."

"Their last name is Tanaka-Ramirez.
They have been married for five years
and want to have a family.
They aren't looking to have a baby yet.
They wanted a child that was old enough to travel
and go on adventures with them first."

"They like adventure? So do I!" I said.

"As I said, this is meant to be,"
said Ms. Boldmore with a twinkle in her eye.
"Now, run along to bed, dear. Tomorrow is a big day."

The tall shadow was in the corner of the room while I was packing my bags. I was worried that it was going to follow me to Will and Harry's just like it has to all the other places that I have lived. I hoped that because I was being adopted, it would finally leave me alone.

"This time is different. I am not going to a foster home. So you can leave me alone now. I have a family that will protect me from you," I whispered to the tall shadow.

I tried not to think about it on the way to Will and Harry's house. I was so excited. But worry and doubt crept into my mind. "What if it never leaves me alone? What if I really am crazy? What if Will and Harry don't want me to be their son anymore? What if... What if everything will turn out great?" That thought helped me feel better.

Chapter Five

Will and Harry's House

Will and Harry's house was nice.
It wasn't very big,
but it looked friendly,
like something from a storybook.
There were trees, flowers,
a blue picket fence and a grassy yard.

"Welcome to your new home, Bentley,"
said Will as he helped me with my big bag.

"We hope you like it," said Harry.

I wanted to say, "Yes, I love it!"
and run around the yard like crazy
but I felt too shy,
like if I talk, I might mess this up.

The house was neat and tidy but not in a way
that made me scared to touch anything.
I could smell something cooking.
The walls were covered with paintings.
There was so much light.
I didn't see the tall shadow anywhere.

"Harry painted all of these," said Will.

"But they won't stay up for long. Those three are sold.
They'll be replaced by new ones soon,"
said Harry.

I wanted to ask Harry questions about painting,
but I just couldn't get any words out yet.
I felt like my awkwardness
was making Will and Harry think
that I didn't want to be here.

"Umm... Lunch will be ready soon," said Will.
"But first, let's get you settled into your room."

At the top of the stairs,
was sort of like a little living room
with a couch and a bookshelf.

"This is the lounge," said Harry.
"You can sit here and read.
We have lots of books.
And we can get more
if we don't have what you like."

I looked at the shelf and tried to smile,
but I was too embarrassed to say that
I didn't really like reading.

"Through that door is the bathroom.
Down the hall is our room.
And here is your room," said Will.

At Ms. Boldmore's,
I had to share a room with other kids.
At the foster homes, the rooms I stayed in
were always decorated with baby stuff.

Will and Harry made this room exactly right for me
with a bed just my size, fresh pillows, and blankets,
a dresser and shelves for my things.
There was even one of Harry's paintings on the wall.
The best part was that they got me my very own desk
with a brand new drawing book and colored pencils.

"Do you like it?" asked Harry.
"If you don't, we can change it.
And that painting doesn't have to stay.
I just thou-"

"Yes," I managed to say
though my voice was quivering from wanting to cry.
"It's perfect."

"You just hang out and relax.
We will call you when lunch is ready," said Will.

Chapter Six
Mr. Flair

Living here didn't feel strange. It was like Will, Harry and the house had been waiting for me all this time, and we finally found each other. We made food and ate together. We told stories and laughed at each other's jokes. Because I was feeling more comfortable to be myself, I started talking more. And I thought about Grace a little less every day.

Harry even made a tree swing in the backyard
for my birthday. The best part of all was that
the tall shadow was nowhere to be seen.

One day, when I was out playing in the yard,
I saw the next-door neighbor.
He was a tall, mysterious looking old man.
I had this strange feeling
like I needed to know more about him.

"Hi," I said waving my hand.
It wasn't like me to be so bold.
"My name is Bentley. I'm your new neighbor."

But the man didn't say hello.
He didn't even stop.
He just walked faster,
pulled his hat tighter to his head,
and grumbled all the way into his dark house.
He slammed the door, and I heard it lock.

I asked Will and Harry about the neighbor.
They said that his name is Mr. Flair.
He is a professor at the same college as Will.
But they have never spoken.
Will said that Mr. Flair doesn't talk to
anyone any more than he has to.

"If he doesn't talk, then how does he teach?" I asked.

"Oh, he is an excellent teacher,
but all of his students are afraid of him," said Will.

"Why?" I asked.

"Because Mr. Flair is actually a *ghost*," said Harry.

My eyes grew wide. "Really?"
I thought of the tall shadow, wondering
what if it had been Mr. Flair all this time.
What if when I got here, he materialized?

"No," said Will nudging Harry. "Mr. Flair is not a ghost.
He is a famous writer."

"What does he write about?" I asked.

"Myths and legends mostly. Some are about adventures,"
said Will.

"Would I like his books?" I asked.

"We can buy a copy and find out.
How does that sound?" said Harry with a smile.

I waited for Mr. Flair to come out of his house.
I wanted to ask him which of his books I should read,
but he never did come outside. It got dark out,
and he didn't even turn on any of his lights.
Then I noticed a sound coming from up high. I looked
up and saw that Mr. Flair was on his roof looking at
the stars through a telescope.

The next day, I saw Mr. Flair walking to his car.
"Mr. Flair, Mr. Flair! It's me, Bentley, your new
neighbor!" I yelled waving to get his attention.
But he only walked faster.

This made him stop.
He glanced at me, and
we studied each other
for a moment. But then,
without a word, he got
in his car and
drove away.
"Nice to meet you too,"
I said sarcastically.

I tore off the paper. "It's a book!" I exclaimed.
"The Adventures of Captain Flair!"

"Mr. Flair gave you a book?" asked Will.
"That's... well, that was very nice of him."

Chapter Seven

I Wonder....?

"My Island, my lighthouse home, it was all I had, but it was not enough. There was nothing left for me here. I needed something more."

Will, Harry and I read
The Adventures of Captain Flair every night before bed. I loved it. It was the story about his life growing up as an orphan on Dawson Island, where he was found as a baby. He sailed to far off lands with his two friends he met along the way.

With nothing but the clothes on my back and the wind in my sails, I set out into the great unknown. Nothing could stop me from finding that treasure. Not my past. Not my fears. Not even the pirates who were after me for stealing their treasure map. No, not even them. I was unstoppable.

Under the cover of night, I sailed the stormy seas.
Dawn was approaching revealing the horizon where
the cave of treasure awaited me.

I loved reading this story.
Even after Will, Harry and I had finished it
I reread it on my own.
It was probably my imagination
but I thought that Captain Flair sorta
kinda looked like me.
He even had a treasure map just like mine.
Our names were almost the same too,
Flair and Fair... It made me wonder.
"What if Mr. Flair was somehow related to me."

Chapter Eight

Chalk Dust

Will and Harry suggested that I try
and make some friends my age.

"Some nice kids live in the neighborhood," said Will.

"There go Sadie and Lewis right now," said Harry,
waving to two kids going by on scooters.
"They kinda remind me of
Captain Flair's friends from the story."

"Daisy Anne and Bright Joe. They were twins." I said.

"Yes, just like Sadie and Lewis.
I think that they're about your age.
Would you like me to introduce you?" asked Will.

"No, no thank you," I said.

Right now I just wanted to be with Will and Harry.
One of my favorite things to do
was chalk drawing out on the sidewalk with them.
Harry was really good.
His chalk art had the same feeling as his paintings.
Will wasn't as good as Harry, but he liked his drawings,
and that's all that mattered.

I drew the map.
I told Will and Harry that Grace was on the island
in a tower, making it a nice place for us to live together.
But I felt like this made Will and Harry
a little uncomfortable.

I changed the subject and told them about how I
thought that this island was the same one as in
The Adventures of Captain Flair.
"Did you notice that Captain Flair even looks like me?
We have the same nose and dark hair."

"I did notice that," said Harry.

"Yeah!" I said, excited that he agreed with me.
"I mean, how many people have hair as
dark and messy as mine?"

"Hello...?" said Will,
pointing to his head of messy black hair.
"You get that mop from me."
We all laughed.

Just then, Mr. Flair came walking by.
He was looking down as usual
and he saw our drawings on the sidewalk.
I hoped that he would notice the map.
And he did.

"You there!...Where did you see this map?"
Mr. Flair asked me.
"You have no right drawing these coordinates out in the
open where anyone could see!"

"Professor Flair, please calm down," said Will.
"Our son did not mean to upset you and he certainly
does not deserve to be spoken to this way."

"You must be mistaken," said Harry.
"This is from Bentley's treasure map.
I don't think that you would have seen it.
It was given to him by his late mother."

"His mother...?" Mr. Flair studied me for a moment
as if he recognized me from another time.
Then he cleared his throat and shook his head.
"Even in chalk dust,
I would recognize this map anywhere.
I drew it myself!"

"I knew it!" I exclaimed, startling everyone.
"Do you still know where the island is?
Is it Dawson Island?
Is the lighthouse really a tower?
Do you remember?"

Mr. Flair glared at me. I could see a hundred thoughts passing through his eyes. I understood now what Will meant about his students being afraid of him, but I didn't back down. I glared just as hard as he did.

Then, just when I thought we would be standing there all day, Mr. Flair took a deep breath and sighed as though he had nothing left to lose.

"Of course I remember," said Mr. Flair, as he knelt beside me to get a better look at the chalk map.

Will and Harry were so surprised they stepped back. I could hear them whispering to each other but I didn't care what they were saying.

"Getting there by land will be easy now. There is a road, and you can drive. In my day, not a soul walked that coastline, except for a stray cow or two," said Mr. Flair pointing along the dots of the chalk map.

"The real map says something about a cave for the split ship," I said. "What does that mean?"

"That is where I left the twin boats. I built them... from another ship," said Mr. Flair. It seemed like a sad memory for him, but I didn't ask why.

"And the lighthouse?" I asked.

"You will see it when you crest the island's hill. However, the real challenge will be the spirit of the island. She protects it," said Mr. Flair.

"Spirit...?" I asked, gulping down my fear.
"Yes..." said Mr. Flair,
seeming to gulp down his trauma.
"She will welcome you only if you are worthy. If not, she will trick your mind into turning back. She will stir up the seas and block your way. She will fill your dreams with haunting nightmares. And she will never let you into the tower."

"I knew that it wasn't a lighthouse!" I said, trying to ignore the fear in my gut. "If it was a lighthouse then the ship that you were on as a baby wouldn't have wrecked! The captain would have seen it and steered clear of the island."
"You are a smart one lad," said Mr. Flair.
"Me, smart...?" I asked.
I had never thought of myself that way.
"Bentley is very smart," declared Will.
"And brave," said Harry.

"I knew that from the moment I saw you," said Mr. Flair. "You will have to be brave. Being the captain of such a mission will take courage."
"Captain... me?" I asked.

"It is in your blood lad. You can do it. And with luck you may even find a treasure," said Mr. Flair.

"Treasure..." I marveled.

"But you will need to go soon." He looked off into the sky. "The winds will be changing with the season, and the seas won't stay calm for much longer," said Mr. Flair before he stood up and walked away.

Chapter Nine

Cave-y

Will and Harry weren't like most people.
They actually listened to me when I spoke.
They knew how important this mission was for me.
Finding Grace would make my family feel complete.
So we got in the car and drove to the sea.

I saw cows behind a fence, and I imagined that they were the ones that Mr. Flair said used to roam free.
"Are you looking out the window, Bentley?"
asked Harry.
"Yep, I see the cows," I said.
"No silly goose. Look the other way. It's the island!"
said Harry.

We parked the car on
the side of the road. I got out my map.
"So that's Dawson Island?" asked Harry.
"Yes, I can sense it," I said.

We walked down to the water.
"There should be a cave around here
somewhere," I said. "It says here that
it is hidden by tall grass."
"It looks kinda cave-y over there,"
said Harry as he started walking
down the beach.

Tucked in the side of the hill
in the tall grass was a cave.
"That's it!" I exclaimed.
"Amazing!" said Will.

Harry went first to check
it out. "Hey, guys, there's
only one boat in here!
I thought you said that
there would be two?"
"Grace must have used
it to get to the island!"
I said excitedly.
"Well, there's only one
way to find out," said Will.

We rowed across the water.
There was no wind or even any waves. But I
felt just like Captain Flair when he was
sailing through the storm on his way to find
the lost treasure. I was Captain Bentley Fair,
on my way to find my lost sister.
"Are you having fun, Bentley?" asked Will.

"Call me Captain," I said
feeling the sea breeze in my face and hair. "And yes!
This is the greatest adventure I have ever had!
I hope the spirit of the island will let us ashore."
"I think that you are already in her favor, Captain.
The seas are calm, and I am not having any crazy
dreams right now," said Harry.

The moment the bow of the boat touched shore I jumped out and ran up the hill.

"Bentley, I mean, Captain wait!" called Harry as he and Will pulled the boat onto the beach so it wouldn't float away. "I need to get a better view!" I yelled.

I stood at the top and I waited for Will and Harry. "This can't be right. I don't see the tower, only trees," I said.

"The spirit of the island isn't letting us see the tower. That's not a good sign," I said.

"Don't worry, Captain. You are safe. Will and I are here with you," said Harry.

"And besides, the island probably wasn't this overgrown the last time Mr. Flair was here. We trust that you can lead the way," said Will.
"You trust me...?" I asked.

"Of course, you are our fearless leader," said Will.

I cleared my throat. "Yes, let's take a look around. I think I see something down there in those trees."

"Oh yeah, I see that too," said Harry.

Chapter Ten

The Island

Exploring the island
felt just like the enchanted jungle in
The Adventures of Captain Flair.
There was no sign of the spirit of the island.
Harry was right. She must want us to be here.

"Look at this tree..." said Harry.

"It's just like the one in the book," said Will.

"That's because it is," I said.

"How do you know?" asked Harry.

"These initials, they are the same ones as in the book,"
I said pointing to the carving.
"Look here: C.F., Captain Flair, B.J., Bright Joe, and D.A.,
Daisy Anne."

The moment I said that last name
I felt a shift in the wind
like someone was waiting for me to say that name.
It caused me to look up, and I saw it.
"The telescope... Captain Flair's telescope!
This was their hideout. I knew it!"

The tower was built of smooth stones from the beach.
We walked around until we found the door.

I tried the handle, but it was locked.

"Hello, is anyone home?" asked Harry
knocking and peering through the window.
"Would you look at this door? the craftsmanship..."

"Harry..." I complained.

"Sorry, Captain," said Harry,
as he looked in the window again.
"I don't think that-"

"Captain! Over here! Take a look at this," said Will.
He was pointing to a secret path to the beach
where the other twin boat
was tucked into the tall grass.

"She is here," I said.
"Grace! Grace, it's me, your brother!" I called out.

"Maybe she isn't inside.
She could be somewhere else on the island,"
said Harry.

We were about to start searching
when the tower door opened.

"Bentley, you came," said Grace.
"Of course I came," I said as I ran to hug her.
"I missed you every day."
"I missed you too. You've gotten so big," said Grace.
"Well, I am 11 now. And you seem bigger too," I said
backing away from our hug.

She laughed nervously."Yes, I have gotten bigger..."
I looked at her with surprise."Are you...?
"Pregnant? Yes, I am." Grace took my hand and placed
it on her tummy. I felt it move like the baby was
trying to get out.

"Are these your new foster parents?" asked Grace looking apprehensively at Will and Harry.
"No," I said. "They aren't my foster parents. This is Will and Harry, and they have adopted me."

I felt like they were worried about something. About Grace's baby? Or maybe Will and Harry thought that I wanted to live with her and not them? They did the nice to meet you's, but I could tell that they were all a little uncomfortable.
"Come in. Let me show you around," said Grace.

Even though it was daytime,
it was dark inside the tower. The stone walls
and windows were gray and murky with grime.
"You have been living here?" asked Will looking
around with concern. "All by yourself?"

"Sort of..."
said Grace.
"I live upstairs.
Let me show
you around."
She led us up
the winding
staircase.

"Are you sure this is safe?" asked Will.
"Oh yeah, I go up and down all the
time and I haven't fallen through yet,"
said Grace.
"It looks fine to me," said Harry
testing the steps with his feet.
"You're the carpenter," said Will.
"But let's all hold hands anyway.
Sound good to you, Captain?"
"Yep!" I said. I was just so happy
that we were all finally together.
"I live at the top, through that
trapdoor," said Grace.

Grace opened the trapdoor
in the ceiling.
She struggled and looked
like she was in pain.
"Let us help you!" said Harry.
"You shouldn't be doing this."
"I'm fine! I do this every day,"
snapped Grace.

"Welcome to my home," said Grace.
"Wow! This is awesome! It's just like I imagined,"
I said as I ran around looking at everything.

Grace had been making this a place to
live. She brought up bottles of water,
soda, and some of our favorite junk
food. She had a bed with extra
pillows and blankets. Only one bed,
but I didn't care if I had to sleep on
the floor. "I love it here! Will, Harry,
can I stay with Grace sometime?"

"Um... Harry and I are going to need to think
about that," said Will. They didn't seem to
think that this place was as cool as I did.

"Bentley can come and stay anytime," said Grace.

"That's very nice, and we will come back soon.
But I think it is time for us to head home for the day,"
said Harry.

"But we just got here," I said.
"I haven't even had a chance to explore
the rest of the island."

"I know, and we will come back soon.
But it is getting late and, Captain
it looks like a storm is coming," said Will
looking out the window.

"Yeah, a storm has been coming
almost every night for the past few days,"
said Grace holding her head.

"Grace, dear you don't look well.
I have to insist that you come back with us.
You can stay at our house for as long as you need,"
said Harry.

"No, I'm fine-ouch!"

Chapter Twelve

The Spirit of the Island

Grace was about to have her baby
and I was scared.
I have taken care of tons of babies
but I have never seen one being born.

"Will she be ok?" I asked.

"Don't worry. Harry knows what to do," said Will
as he collected all of the bottled water.

"My mom is a nurse. When I was little,
she would take me with her on her rounds,"
said Harry as he gathered extra blankets.

"What should I do?" I asked.

"You can help me-"

"No!" Grace snapped interrupting Harry.
"I don't want Bentley to see me like this."

I waited at the top of the stairs.
The storm grew on the horizon
and swept across the sea.
The wind and rain beat against the windows.
And on top of that, the tall shadow was back.

I wondered if it had followed me here.
Or, what if the tall shadow was really
the spirit of the island?
Did she bring this storm upon us because she didn't
want us here? I was terrified.

I wished that Ms. Boldmore were here.
She would know just what to say to keep me calm.
She would tell me to try some
"what ifs".

"What if Grace and her baby are going to be fine?
What if they move into Will and Harry's house
and we all live happily ever after?
What if the spirit of the island
is good and she is looking out for us?
What if since my whole family is together
she will finally leave me alone?"

"What if I trust that everything
will turn out all right?"
I tried saying this out loud to the tall shadow.

"I am safe. You can leave me alone now.
Everything will turn out fine."
The shadow seemed to be listening.
From the corner of my eye, she appeared
to change just a little. I could almost see
her face. But before I could tell who
she was, I heard a baby cry.

"What are you going to name him?" I asked.
"I don't know," Grace said flatly.

"Can I help you decide?" I asked.
"Sure," she said like she didn't care.
"Are you feeling ok?" I asked.
"I'm fine, just tired. Here, you hold him,"
she said handing me the baby.
He was so small and perfect. "I love you,
little one, whatever your name is," I said.

Chapter Thirteen

Heartbroken

"I am not ready to be a mother. Will and Harry, you guys are better parents than I could ever be. Bentley will help you with the baby. He will make a good big brother. I'm sorry, Grace."

"Why?" I asked holding the key in my hand.

"I...I don't know. I'm so sorry, Bentley." said Will.

"I'm sorry too, sweetheart. But we have to leave. We need to get this little guy some food," said Harry.

We went back through the woods
the same way that we came.
I hoped that Grace would see
that she made a mistake
and be waiting for us at the boat.

I felt so frustrated and confused.
I didn't understand why she had to leave
right when the whole family finally came together.
I had this strange feeling that I should look back.
I hoped it was Grace, but it wasn't.
It was the tall shadow.

"No, it's following us," I thought.
I was about to tell Will and Harry
that we needed to hurry when, before my eyes,
the tall shadow shifted into an old woman.
She floated into the light and waved to me.
The spirit of the island... I realized.
She had been the tall shadow this whole time,
looking out for me, waiting
until I was ready to show who she truly was.

"Daisy Anne..." I said.

"What's that, Captain?" asked Will.

"Nothing," I said.
"It's all right. Everything is going to be all right."

As Harry rowed us all back to shore,
Will had me sit next to him on the floor of the boat.
He said that it would make it safer for the baby.
I cried the whole way back.
So did the little guy.
But I was still able to help comfort him.

"Do you have any ideas for a name?" asked Will.

"We could call him Captain," said Harry.

"Oh no, that's Bentley's title," said Will.

"What about Dawson?" I said.

"Dawson...? I like it," said Harry.
"How did you come up with it?"

"The island," I said.

"That's right, Dawson Island.
What do you say, little one...?"
Will asked the baby.

He smiled just a little and then burped.

"He likes it," I said.

We drove straight to Ms. Boldmore's.
She was very surprised to see us with
a baby. We told her what had happened
and how Grace had left Dawson to us.

"Did Grace tell you that she was going to have a baby?" I asked.

"No, not in so many words, but I had a feeling," said Ms. Boldmore.

"She shouldn't have left for the island if she knew that she was going to have a baby. That was a mistake," I said.

"None of this was a mistake, my dear," said Ms. Boldmore. "Dawson was meant for this family." She gave us a diaper bag full of supplies for Dawson with everything he would need until tomorrow when we could go to the store ourselves.

"You call me anytime if you need anything. But you are in good hands with Captain Bentley," she said as she gave me a hug.

Chapter Fourteen

Grandfather

Settling Dawson into the house felt good.
It was like he had always been here.
I was still sad about Grace leaving him though.

"What is it, sweetheart?" asked Harry.

"I'm sad that Grace won't get to watch Dawson grow.
It's only been a week, and
he has already gotten bigger.
What if Dawson misses her?" I asked.

"Well... do you miss your mother?" asked Will.

I thought about it for a moment.
"I never knew her.
Grace missed her, and that made me sad."

"Do you think that Dawson wants you to be sad
missing Grace for him?" asked Will.

"No, he just wants everyone to be happy," I said
as Dawson touched my face with his little hand.

One day, I saw Mr. Flair walking by.
I realized that I hadn't told him about
my adventure on the island.

I grabbed the map, telescope,
and key and I ran outside to
catch up with him.
"Mr. Flair, Mr. Flair! I did it. I
followed the map and found
the tower on the island."

I told him about Grace and Dawson too. "And here, I thought that you might want these back. I found the telescope in the lookout tree. It's the one from your story isn't it?" I asked handing him back the telescope and key.

"Haha. I haven't seen those in... well, a long time," said Mr. Flair, but he didn't take them from me. "What of the spirit of the island? Did she lead you to the treasure?"

I was about to run back in the house to tell Will, Harry, and Dawson about the treasure, but I had to ask about something that had been churning in my mind.

"Mr. Flair? I've been meaning to ask you... the map and the telescope from the book, the way that you said, 'what's now rightfully mine.' Even our names, Flair and Fair, are almost the same... Mr. Flair, are you... are you my grandfather?"

But when I turned around
Mr. Flair had gone.
And he didn't come back.

Chapter Fifteen

More Adventure to Come

One day, a package arrived
from Ms. Boldmore. It was the box
that she had given to Grace on her 18th birthday.
On that day, Grace had only shown me the map and
the key. Now, I got to see what else was inside.

The box contained another map and key
that looked even older than the first ones.
There was also a letter from my mother.
It said that Grace and I had a grandfather.
And that she had changed our name to Fair
because she didn't want us to know about him yet.
But she wished that we could meet him one day.
His name is Igor Flair.

Will and Harry tried to track down Mr. Flair. But
Will said that Mr. Flair had left his teaching position
to resume his writing career.

I was sad about not being able
to talk to Mr. Flair anymore.
I had so many more questions to ask him.

Was the spirit of the island actually Daisy Anne?
If so, what happened to her?
Did she die?
Was she my grandmother?
Since Mr. Flair could see her,
did that mean that he could see spirits too,
just like me?

He was the only real friend
that I had ever made and now he was gone.

I saw Sadie and Lewis outside playing.
They didn't seem so bad.
Maybe I will go and say hi sometime.

But not right now.
Right now, I am drawing.

"Do you think that Ms. Boldmore was right?"
I asked Will and Harry.

"About what, sweetheart?" asked Will.

"She said that the way our family
came together was meant to be."

"I believe her," said Harry.

"But what about Grace and Mr. Flair?
They are part of this family too," I said.

"Well, Bentley," said Will.
"The way I see it,
some people are in your life for a reason."

"Like Grace? Her reason was giving us Dawson,"
I said.

"That's right," said Will.
"And others are only here for a season."

"Like Mr. Flair?" I said.

"Yes, just like Mr. Flair," said Harry.

"But what about you two and Dawson?" I asked.

"You've got us for a lifetime," said Will.

The End

About the Author

Mary B. Truly is an American author and illustrator.
She grew up in the rolling hills of
Freeland, Maryland
and has traveled all over the U.S.
There have been very few times when
Mary has not had a drawing book and
colored pencils by her side.
She has always dreamed of creating children's books
filled with love, kindness, and adventure.

CPSIA information can be obtained
at www.ICGtesting.com
Printed in the USA
BVHW092224040522
636049BV00003B/23